TOO MANY PUMPKINS

Linda White

illustrated by Megan Lloyd

Holiday House/New York

For Aunt Becky, who cooked the pumpkins,
and Daddy and Uncle Fred, who ate them.
L. W.

To Sara and Steve,
two who have been waiting
too long for this dedicating!
M.L.

Text copyright © 1996 by Linda White
Illustrations copyright © 1996 by Megan Lloyd-Thompson
All rights reserved
Printed and bound in April 2021 at Toppan Leefung, DongGuan City, China.
28

Library of Congress Cataloging-in-Publication Data
White, Linda, 1948–
Too many pumpkins / Linda White ; illustrated by Megan Lloyd. —

p.   cm.
Summary: Rebecca Estelle, an old woman who has hated pumpkins ever
since she was a girl and her family had nothing else to eat, finds
herself with a full crop of them.

[1. Pumpkins—Fiction. 2. Friendship—Fiction.] I. Lloyd,
Megan, ill. II. Title.
PZ7.W58385To   1996   95-45376   CIP   AC
[Fic—dc20]

ISBN-13: 978-0-8234-1245-7 (hardcover)   ISBN-10: 0-8234-1245-8 (hardcover)
ISBN-13: 978-0-8234-1320-1 (paperback)   ISBN-10: 0-8234-1320-9 (paperback)

Every year at springtime, Rebecca Estelle planted just enough seeds in her garden to grow vegetables for the long winter. She planted carrots and beans, tomatoes and peas, corn and rutabagas. She grew a little bit of everything— except pumpkins.

Rebecca Estelle *hated* pumpkins!

When she was a little girl, money had been scarce. For an entire month, all there had been to eat were pumpkins. Baked pumpkins, steamed pumpkins, boiled pumpkins. Stewed pumpkins, mashed pumpkins, rotten pumpkins. Breakfast pumpkins, lunch pumpkins, dinner pumpkins. Enough pumpkins!

When things finally improved and there was more money to buy food, Rebecca Estelle decided she would never eat pumpkins again. Or even *look* at one. Not ever.

And she didn't, until . . .

. . . one autumn day long after Rebecca Estelle's hair had turned snowy white. She was raking the leaves that fell each fall from her black walnut tree, and her cat, Esmeralda, was scattering them just as quickly. All of a sudden, the pumpkin truck passed by.

Oh, she heard it coming. And she knew what it was. It rumbled by at harvesttime every year. She turned her back and concentrated on picking up the last fallen leaf.

She managed to ignore the truck, until . . .

SPLAT! An enormous pumpkin tumbled off the truck and smashed into slimy orange smithereens all over the edge of her yard.

"Come back here and get this pumpkin," she yelled. But the driver sped away.

"Well, I won't touch it," Rebecca Estelle insisted, getting her shovel from the barn.

"And I won't look at it," she added as she shoveled dirt on top of the pumpkin pieces.

"I won't *think* about that pumpkin ever again," she declared.

And she didn't, until . . .

"Well, I won't touch it," Rebecca Estelle insisted, getting her shovel from the barn.

"And I won't look at it," she added as she shoveled dirt on top of the pumpkin pieces.

"I won't *think* about that pumpkin ever again," she declared.

And she didn't, until . . .

. . . spring when Rebecca Estelle was admiring the new sprouts in her garden. She noticed Esmeralda playing in some big green leaves growing at the edge of the yard. "How curious," she said, going over to inspect them. "I didn't plant anything there."

Then Rebecca Estelle remembered the pumpkin truck and the slimy pumpkin smithereens.

"Pumpkins!" she cried in disgust. "Come out of there, Esmeralda. I will not water those plants. I will not tend them. I will ignore them and they will die."

She picked up Esmeralda and stomped inside. But a week later, when Rebecca Estelle peered out her window, she saw that the vines had grown.

She tramped to the barn, got her garden tools, and went to work on the pumpkin vines. She cut and dug until not one was left growing.

"There, now there will be no pumpkins." She smiled and went back inside.

But the next week, when she was weeding the garden, she noticed that the pumpkin vines had grown back. Rebecca Estelle marched inside and snapped the curtains shut. "The only thing to do is ignore them. They won't grow if I don't take care of them," she muttered. So, rain or shine, all spring and summer, she never looked out the front window. She used only the back door and never even glanced toward the vines. Neither did Esmeralda.

Rebecca Estelle ignored the vines so well that, in time she forgot why she wasn't using the front door, until . . .

one autumn day, when she and Esmeralda went to rake the leaves that fell each fall from the black walnut tree in front of the house.

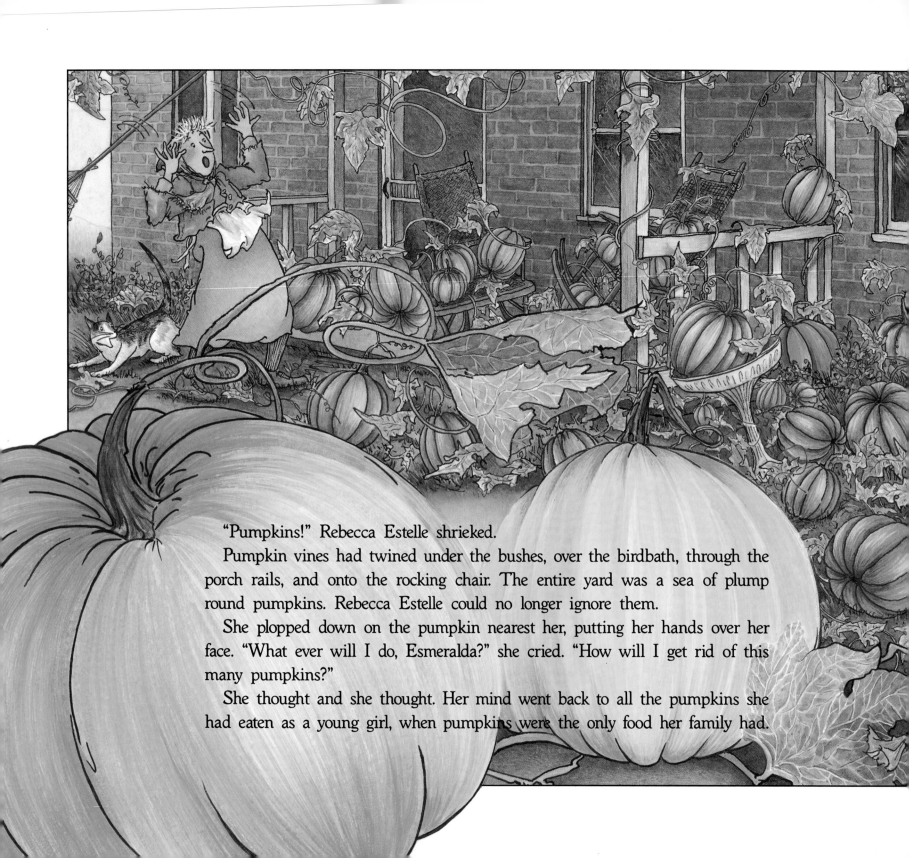

"Pumpkins!" Rebecca Estelle shrieked.

Pumpkin vines had twined under the bushes, over the birdbath, through the porch rails, and onto the rocking chair. The entire yard was a sea of plump round pumpkins. Rebecca Estelle could no longer ignore them.

She plopped down on the pumpkin nearest her, putting her hands over her face. "What ever will I do, Esmeralda?" she cried. "How will I get rid of this many pumpkins?"

She thought and she thought. Her mind went back to all the pumpkins she had eaten as a young girl, when pumpkins were the only food her family had.

"Well, we can't let them stay here," she told Esmeralda. "Some people might need these pumpkins, and I suppose there are folks crazy enough to like them. We'll *give* them away." She marched off to get her wheelbarrow.

Rebecca Estelle struggled to lift the first pumpkin, then the second and the third. She huffed and she puffed as she wheeled the loaded wheelbarrow into the lane.

"I'm too tired to deliver these heavy pumpkins now," Rebecca Estelle grumbled. She mopped her brow with her apron and wondered what to do next.

"Perhaps if I make them into pies, they will be easier to deliver. Such a nuisance!"

So she went to work. She scooped the slimy seeds out of the pumpkins and cut away the shells. After she boiled the pumpkin meat, she mixed it with eggs, milk, sugar, flour, cinnamon, nutmeg, and cloves to make rich pies. Then Rebecca Estelle made pumpkin tarts, pumpkin muffins, pumpkin cakes. Pumpkin bread, pumpkin pudding, pumpkin cookies, until . . .

. . . pumpkin dishes spilled out of every cupboard, drawer, and cubbyhole, and the seeds were a mountain in the corner.

"Well, that's the first batch," Rebecca Estelle said, dusting her floury hands. "Now to deliver them."

She put the wheelbarrow outside the kitchen door, then loaded it with pumpkin treats. When it was full, just the *thought* of delivering all those pumpkin dishes made Rebecca Estelle tired. "If only people would come get them," she said.

Then she had an idea. Rebecca Estelle whirled around and hurried back into the house for a kitchen knife.

"This should get people to come," Rebecca Estelle cried.

She took her knife and sat in the middle of the pumpkin patch. She carved a smiling face on a nice round pumpkin, a scary snaggletoothed face on a tall thin pumpkin, and "BOO!" on a short squat pumpkin. She was so busy carving pumpkins, she hardly noticed how dark it was getting. When she could no longer see, she went to the shelf on the back porch and got the sack of candles she kept for emergencies.

"If this doesn't get people to come here, we'll have to deliver them all ourselves," she muttered to Esmeralda.

Rebecca Estelle peered into the darkness for a long time. She didn't see anything. Still, she watched, until . . .

finally she saw a light, faint at first, then
brighter, and then more lights bobbing through the night. "Here they come," she
shouted. "Esmeralda, let's heat some apple cider."

Young and old, everyone in town came.

"Rebecca Estelle, we thought you hated pumpkins," they said. "We saw your jack-o'-lanterns from the end of the road and came for a closer look."

"I was hoping you would," said Rebecca Estelle.

"Where did you ever find all these pumpkins?" people asked.

"I came by them quite by accident," Rebecca Estelle said, smiling. "Would you like some pumpkin pie? There's plenty." She winked at Esmeralda. Everyone enjoyed the pumpkin pie and cider and had a good time. So did Rebecca Estelle. And when they were ready to go home, she made sure each carried a jack-o'-lantern, a bag of seeds for roasting, and a pumpkin treat. Rebecca Estelle gave away everything that reminded her of the pumpkins she had always hated, until . . .

. . . all that remained was a handful of seeds.

Those she tucked snugly into her pocket, where they would be safe until planting time next spring.